Planet Kayteru

The Flying

A Black Hole

The Space Giant's
Beanstalk

Major Tom

Oddball

Series 814

The Fun Guys Stories:

The Spring Time and the Moth Ball
The Hen Coat and the Ship Shape
The Rat Race and the Sky Lark
The Bottleneck and the Mole Hole
The Mush Rooms and the Fox Glove
The Mouse Trap and the Cricket Team

The Adventures of Major Tom:

The Planet of the Elves
The Missing Ambassador
The Space Pirates

First Edition

Adventures of Major Tom
The Missing Ambassador

written and illustrated by PETER LONGDEN

Ladybird Books Loughborough

Major Tom and his robot assistant, Oddball, were travelling through space in their flying orange. They were off on another very important mission.

"Here we are!" shouted Oddball, as the flying orange went into orbit around the planet Glukonia.

5

Earlier, back on earth, base control had had an urgent call from the Glukons. These were the friendly creatures who lived on the planet and they needed help. Base control had ordered Tom to go and see what was wrong.

Now they were here. Tom and Oddball got out of their spaceship.

A very worried little Glukon came over to meet them.

"Major Tom at your service, sir," said Tom. "Can you tell me what's wrong?"

"Oh I'm so glad you're here. Our Ambassador has been kidnapped," said the Glukon. "He's been taken to the Red Planet and the evil Scorpion is demanding every bit of our glukonite in exchange for the safe return of our Ambassador."

Glukonite was mined on the planet Glukonia. It was highly explosive and would be very dangerous in the wrong hands. "This is very serious," thought Tom.

9

Tom and Oddball knew that every
planet in the galaxy was in danger.
They had to rescue the Ambassador
quickly. So once again Tom was back
in the orange with Oddball steering it
towards the Red Planet.

They had been on their way for some time when Oddball said, "I think we've got company, Major."

"Switch on the televiewer," ordered Tom.

There on the screen was a strange-looking spacecraft and it was closing in on the flying orange.

Before Tom could increase speed, a
porthole opened in the side of the
enemy spacecraft. As Tom and Oddball
watched, huge ants began flying
towards the orange.

"Looks like the Scorpion's army," said
Tom. "Let's get out of here, Oddball."

But it was too late. Within seconds the
orange was surrounded.

"Stand by for attack!" shouted Tom.

"Just a minute, Major! I've got an idea," interrupted Oddball.

"Let's hear it, Oddball. There isn't much time," said Tom, as the ants continued to surround the orange.

"Well, sir, why don't we let them capture us and take us to the Scorpion? That way we'll find the enemy *and* the Ambassador," explained Oddball.

"That's a good idea!" agreed Tom. So they allowed the ants to force them down on to the Red Planet.

They landed on one of the strange lakes and, as they bobbed up and down on the water, Tom and Oddball wondered what would happen next.

Unseen by Tom and Oddball, the
Scorpion had been watching. He
laughed as he thought about what he
was going to do to the famous Major
Tom. Then suddenly everyone's
thoughts were interrupted as the
surface of the lake began to bubble.

This was followed by a huge explosion as an enormous, ugly, green, scaly monster rose up out of the water. It twisted and turned and thrashed about until its eyes settled on the orange, bobbing about close by.

It was dinner-time and the creature was hungry. The monster began to move closer and closer to the orange.

Tom and Oddball had no idea what was going on, so Oddball turned on the orange's televiewer.

''Oh no!'' yelled Tom, as he saw what was outside.

As the monster's great jaws opened, Oddball realised what was about to happen.

"Quick! Fast dive, Major!"
cried Oddball. Tom pounced
on the superdive button.

As the monster's teeth
snapped shut, Tom and
Oddball were diving, at top
speed, deep down into the
lake.

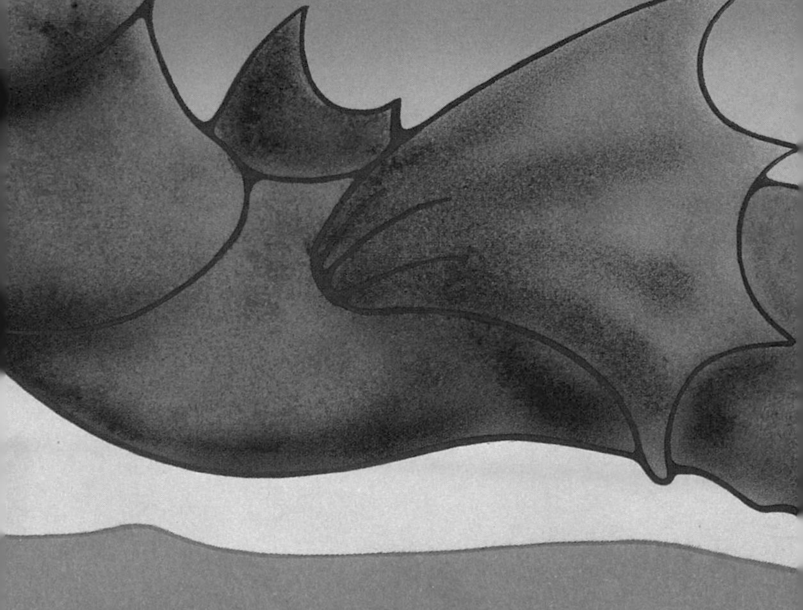

They reached the bottom of the lake.

"Cut engines," ordered Tom.

"Phew! That was a narrow escape," said Oddball.

"Don't speak too soon," said Tom, pointing to a strange-looking fish, making signs at them through the porthole.

"He wants us to follow him," said Oddball.

So Tom and Oddball started the engines once again and followed the little fish through the water. They came to the surface in a large underground cave.

"Up viewing tower," shouted Tom. "Let's take a careful look round this time."

The two were amazed at what they saw. Beautiful flowers hung down from dazzling white rocks and the floor glowed with a blue light.

The little fish, who had been their guide, was soon joined by others.

One of them came up to the spacecraft. "I am the leader of the Fish People," he said. "Don't be afraid, we are your friends. Come out and meet everyone."

So Tom and Oddball climbed out of the orange and were made very welcome in the beautiful city of the Fish People. Tom told them all about the Glukons and the Scorpion.

"We need to rescue the Ambassador quickly," Tom ended his story.

"We'll help you," said the chief fish. "The Scorpion is no friend of ours."

"We can show you an underground passage which leads straight into the Scorpion's den," said the fish. "But you will need to get past the ant guards."

Oddball was thinking. "We could do with some sort of disguise," he said. "Just a minute. I've remembered something." And he rushed back to the orange.

Oddball came back with a huge bundle. "I knew this would come in useful one day. Try it on, Major."

"What is it?" asked Tom.

"It's a giant ant-eater costume and there's room for both of us. It's just what we need to get past the Scorpion's ant guards," said Oddball.

The Fish People took Tom and Oddball down the underground passage. "Good luck!" they whispered, before they went back to their own city.

The ant-eater trotted quietly towards the guards. Then one of them suddenly saw it coming.

"Help! Run for your lives. It's the dreaded giant ant-eater. We'll be eaten alive!" screamed the ant guards, as they rushed away in all directions.

Soon the way was clear for Tom and Oddball to walk straight into the Scorpion's den.

"I told you it would work!" whispered Oddball, from the back end of the costume.

Everywhere was very quiet. Tom and Oddball crept behind some rocks and climbed out of the costume. Then they took a good look round.

"Look! Over there!" hissed Oddball. "It's the Ambassador."

"You're right," said Tom, as he spotted the old Glukon tied up to a huge pole.

Tom took a deep breath and looked all around for signs of danger. Then he crept out from his hiding place and tiptoed over to the Ambassador, who looked very frightened.

So far, so good. Tom began to untie the rope round the Ambassador.

"Don't be afraid," he whispered. "I'm Major Tom and I'm here to rescue you, but we haven't much time. We scared the guards away but they'll soon realise it was a trick."

The Ambassador tried to smile but Tom had hardly finished speaking when they heard the sound of terrible, spine-chilling laughter.

The ant guards had been led back by their leader — the Scorpion.

As the guards flew round Tom, the Scorpion stood laughing.

Tom turned to face his enemy as the terrible creature said, "My plan worked. I knew you would come here in the end." Then he snapped at his guards, "Tie him up!"

Now both the Ambassador *and* Tom were tied to the pole. The guards flew round them, pleased to have captured the one who had tricked them with that ant-eater costume.

All this time, Oddball had been watching from behind the rocks. He needed another good idea. He alone would have to rescue the Ambassador and Major Tom.

Oddball *did* have an idea and he hurried back along the secret passage to the Fish People. He told them what had happened and then rushed off to the flying orange. He flew back in Segment One, the high-speed mini-ship, and, with a quick wave to the Fish People, he zoomed back to the Scorpion's den.

By the time Oddball got there it was dark and the guards had gone. The Scorpion was about to send a message to Glukonia and tell them that he would get rid of both their Ambassador *and* Major Tom if they didn't send all their glukonite at once.

Oddball had stopped right over the two prisoners. Tom heard the hum of the engine as Segment One's mechanical arm was lowered on to the pole.

Tom watched as Oddball then put the ship into reverse. He revved the engines and with a mighty pull, lifted the pole, with its two prisoners still tied on, into the air.

The noise had brought the Scorpion back but he was too late.

Oddball flew them back to the safety of the Fish People. The Ambassador was so pleased to be free. "Now we won't have to give the glukonite to that wicked Scorpion. Thank you, Major Tom," he said.

49

"It was nothing," replied Tom.
"Oddball is the real hero. Without him,
who knows what the Scorpion might
have done to us!"

That night, after they had said goodbye
to the Fish People, Major Tom and
Oddball flew back to Glukonia with the
Ambassador on board. The Glukons
were very happy to see him safely
home.

And so Tom and Oddball left the planet
and set off through space once more.

They knew it wouldn't be too long
before base control sent them on
another mission.

51